You Can Do It Too!

Karen Baicker

pictures by Ken Wilson-Max

Handprint Books 🖐 Brooklyn, New York

We can **star** in our **own** band. I'll **BANG** the pot, you **CLANK** the pan.

You Can Do It Too!

Just for you,
as a favor,

You Can Do It Too!

and see the world
from
upside
down.

Look at what
I'm doing
NOW!
I'm so proud
YOU showed ME
HOW!

YoU Can Do It Too!